10 Stories to Make a Difference is a collection of ten original illustrated stories for young readers, all inspired by the theme of *difference*. The collection features a mix of well-known and emerging writers and illustrators, giving a platform to untold stories and diverse new voices. Produced by Pop Up Projects, a non-profit, UK-based national children's literature development agency, 10 Stories celebrates Pop Up's 10th birthday in 2021. Proceeds from sales supports Pop Up's work in deprived schools, marginalised communities, and with talented writers and illustrators, especially from backgrounds that are under-represented in children's publishing. 10 Stories will be an annual publishing event, with a whole new collection planned for 2022.

Find out more at **www.pop-up.org.uk**

Eleanor Cullen writes fun, rhyming stories, enjoys designing cross-stitch patterns in her spare time, and lives in New Brighton with her canine writing companion. After graduating from Liverpool John Moores University with a BA in English and Creative Writing, she's currently studying for her MA. Eleanor was one of four young winners of Pop Up's 10th Birthday Writing Competition in 2020; *A Match for a Mermaid* was chosen out of 100s of entries from 40 countries, and is Eleanor's first published children's book.

David Roberts studied fashion design at college before becoming a children's book illustrator. His many illustrated books include the New York Times number 1 bestsellers *Sofia Valdez, Future Prez* and *Ada Twist, Scientist* as well as *Dirty Bertie*, *The Cook and the King* (with Julia Donaldson) and *The Bolds* (with Julian Clary).

Edited by **Libby Hamilton**, Andersen Press
Art directed by **Jane Buckley**, Simon & Schuster

Publisher **Dylan Calder**
Coordinator **Amanda Saakwa-Mante**
Designer **Txabi Jones**

A Match for a Mermaid

written by
Eleanor Cullen
illustrated by
David Roberts

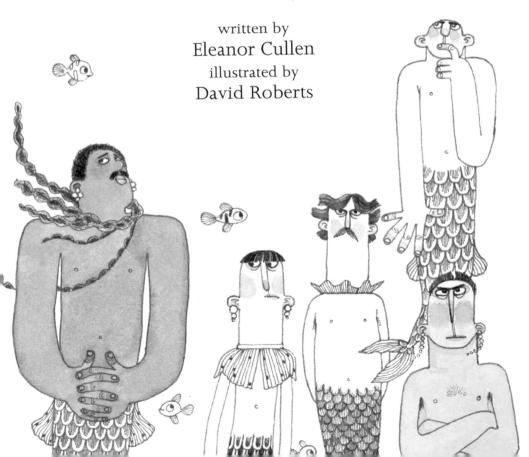

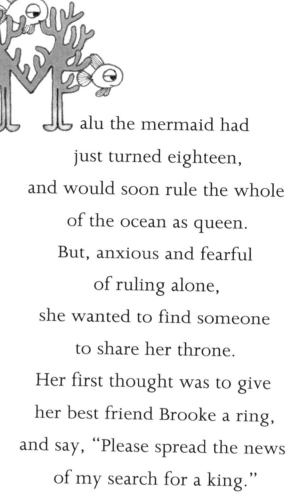 alu the mermaid had
just turned eighteen,
and would soon rule the whole
of the ocean as queen.
But, anxious and fearful
of ruling alone,
she wanted to find someone
to share her throne.
Her first thought was to give
her best friend Brooke a ring,
and say, "Please spread the news
of my search for a king."

And so, Brooke did as
she was told to do,
repeating the news to
all mermen she knew.

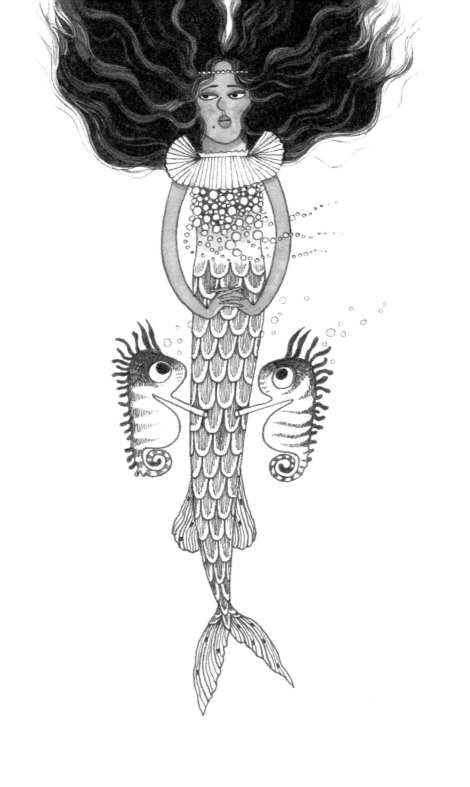

ermen came to meet Malu
from all over the ocean,
there were so many of them,
they caused a commotion!
Each brought a present
for their future queen,
and as they waited their turn,
they would pout, primp and preen.

Malu called up the first,
with his stylish new haircut,
"Hello Princess Malu,
I am Baron Turbot."

He waited before her
and so did the crowd.
They waited and waited,
till she spoke aloud.

"Thank you for coming,
and for the gift too,
but… your hair is too short
so I can't marry you."

The whole line of mermen
heard what she had said,
and one by one started
to check their own head.
Each worried and whined
that their hair wasn't right,

and then swam away,
out of Malu's sight.
"Brooke," said the princess.
"Once more please – your aid.
Bring me a king
who has hair I can braid."

And so, Brooke did as
she was told to do,
repeating the wish
to all merfolk she knew.

Next day brought new mermen,
with hair down their back,
and again each one carried
a gift or knick-knack.
But, waiting in line,
they were messing about;
so loud and unruly
they started to shout.

Malu called up the first man,
his voice deep and low,
"Hello there, princess,
I'm Captain Nemo."

He waited before her
and so did the crowd.
They waited and waited
till she spoke aloud.

"Thank you for coming,
and for the gift too,
But… your voice is too gruff
so I can't marry you."

All other mermen
had heard this rebuff,
and one by one checked
if their voices were gruff.
Each grumbled and groused
that their voice wasn't right,

then swam away quickly,
out of Malu's sight.
"Brooke," said the princess,
"I'm almost heartbroken.
Please bring me men
who are kind and soft spoken."

So again, Brooke did as
she was told to do,
repeating the wish
to all creatures she knew.

Next day brought fresh mermen,
with voices quite mild.
There were less of them now,
so they all laughed and smiled.
As they waited in line,
they murmured together,
each voice as hushed
as a floating white feather.

The first was so quiet,
Brooke spoke up instead:
"For you, Princess Malu,
this is Duke Turtlehead."

He snorted and giggled,
then so did the crowd.
They waited and waited
till she spoke aloud.

"Thank you for coming,
and for the gift too,
but you laugh with a snort
so I can't marry you."

The other mermen
had all heard her complain,
and they couldn't believe
she was moaning again.
It seemed like she'd always find
something not right,

so they all swam away,
out of Malu's sight.
"Oh Brooke," sighed the princess,
"I made them all sad.
Please find me a king
whose laugh won't drive me mad."

And so, Brooke did as
she was told to do.
She repeated Malu's wish
to everyone she knew.

ext day brought one merman;

he was all that remained.

Having heard about each suitor,

he looked very drained.

But his voice was soft

and his hair was long,

and he'd been told many times

his laugh was like song.

Everyone knew that

he was a good catch,

and said that this would be

an excellent match.

Brooke called up the man,

and said with a sigh,

"For you, Princess Malu,

this is King Kai."

So he waited before her,
and so did the crowd.
He waited and waited
till she spoke aloud.
She said, "Thank you for coming,
and for the gift too,
but your face is too rough
so I can't marry you."

And so Kai swam off,
clearly in despair,
as Malu turned to Brooke -
the last person there.
"Now what do I do?"
she gloomily said,
"There's no man in the ocean
who I want to wed."

t this, Brooke looked nervous
and took Malu's hand.
She gazed at her and gave
the speech she had planned.

"I like to think that
my face isn't rough,
and I do not shout,
so my voice isn't gruff.
You can see for yourself
that my hair isn't short,
and if something is funny,
I don't laugh with a snort.
I don't have a gift,
and I don't have a jewel,
but if you married me,
I'd help you to rule."

After Brooke spoke,
Malu started to smile.
It turned to a grin
and she laughed for a while.

"Your hair is flowing
and as smooth as silk,
your laugh is lyrical
and I love its lilt.
Your face is my favourite
and your voice is too;
it would be a great honour
to marry you."

Malu the mermaid
has just turned eighteen,
and with her wife Brooke
they now rule as two queens.

The end

For Lilia, George and Freddie (Eleanor)

This book is dedicated to you, its reader, with love (David)

Thank You!

The 10 Stories collection has been made possible through the generosity and love poured into these stories by our old friends and new, the writers and illustrators who all gave their wisdom and magic: Philip Ardagh, Avital Balwit, Jamie Beard, Sita Brahmachari, Eleanor Cullen, Danica Da Silva Pereira, Ria Dastidar, Alexis Deacon, Laura Dockrill, Jamila Gavin, Sahar Haghgoo, Jay Hulme, Daniel Ido, Krista M. Lambert, Jane Ray, Jacinta Read, Chris Riddell, David Roberts, Marcus Sedgwick, Anjali Tiwari. And through the kindness and devotion of the brilliant publishing editors, art directors and designers who volunteered their time to transform these great stories into even greater books: Emily Ball, Liz Bankes, Andrew Biscomb, Jane Buckley, Alice Curry, Holly Fulbrook, Lilly Gottwald, Elorine Grant, Libby Hamilton, Daisy Jellicoe, Txabi Jones, Ruth Knowles, Tiffany Leeson, Jacqui McDonough, Caroline Royds, Chloé Tartinville, Holly Tonks, Clare Whitston, Sean Williams. Huge gratitude to Matt Baxter and Lydia Fisher at Baxter & Bailey for donating their time to produce the 10 Stories brand, style and formats. If it wasn't for the 643 donors to our crowdfunding campaign, these books may never have made it to print - and we especially want to thank Rachel Denwood and Simon & Schuster, Sam Arthur and Nobrow, Michelle McLeod and Baillie Gifford, the CSR team at Linklaters LLP, Tim Bevan, Wolfgang Tillmans and all our former Board members for their generous support. Behind the scenes, the team and Board at Pop Up kept this great ship afloat through these most turbulent times, and we cannot thank them enough for always being part of the story no matter how hard the story gets.

Made possible by

 Baxter & Bailey  SIMON & SCHUSTER